W9-CKU-929

# Legion of Lava

By Jordan Quinn
Illustrated by Ornella Greco at Glass House Graphics

LITTLE SIMON
New York London Toronto Sydney New Delhi

This book is a work of fiction. Any references to historical events, real people, or real places are used fictitiously. Other names, characters, places, and events are products of the author's imagination, and any resemblance to actual events or places or persons, living or dead, is entirely coincidental.

LITTLE SIMON
An imprint of Simon & Schuster Children's Publishing Division
1230 Avenue of the Americas, New York, New York 10020
First Little Simon edition April 2023.  LITTLE SIMON is a registered trademark of Simon & Schuster, Inc., and associated colophon is a trademark of Simon & Schuster, Inc. For information about special discounts for bulk purchases, please contact Simon & Schuster Special Sales at 1-866-506-1949 or business@simonandschuster.com. The Simon & Schuster Speakers Bureau can bring authors to your live event. For more information or to book an event, contact the Simon & Schuster Speakers Bureau at 1-866-248-3049 or visit our website at www.simonspeakers.com. Text by Matthew J. Gilbert. GLASS HOUSE GRAPHICS Creative Services. Art and cover by ORNELLA GRECO. Colors by ORNELLA GRECO and GABRIELE CRACOLICI. Lettering by GIOVANNI SPATARO/Grafimated Cartoon. Supervision by SALVATORE DI MARCO/Grafimated Cartoon. Manufactured in China 1222 SCP · 2 4 6 8 10 9 7 5 3 1 · Library of Congress Cataloging-in-Publication Data. Names: Quinn, Jordan, author. | Glass House Graphics, illustrator. Title: Legion of lava / by Jordan Quinn ; illustrated by Glass House Graphics. Description: First Little Simon edition. | New York : Little Simon, 2023. | Series: Dragon kingdom of Wrenly ; 9 | Audience: Ages 5-9. | Summary: "Cinder has left to find the truth about Villinelle, while the others are on the hunt for Valos, the evil wizard who is out to destroy all of dragonkind with beasts born from the fiery depths of Crestwood."—Provided by publisher. | Identifiers: LCCN 2022031418 (print) | LCCN 2022031419 (ebook) | ISBN 9781665904612 (paperback) | ISBN 9781665904629 (hardcover) | ISBN 9781665904636 (ebook) | Subjects: LCSH: Graphic novels. | CYAC: Graphic novels. | Dragons—Fiction. | Good and evil—Fiction. | Friendship—Fiction. | LCGFT: Graphic novels. | Classification: LCC PZ7.7.Q55 Le 2023 (print) | LCC PZ7.7.Q55 (ebook) | DDC 741.5/973—dc23/eng/20220909 | LC record available at https://lccn.loc.gov/2022031418 | LC ebook record available at https://lccn.loc.gov/2022031419

# Contents

Chapter 1
The search was on.

SNIFF
SNIFF
By land.

By sea.

ZIIIIIP
And by air.

Our heroes worked tirelessly to scout every corner of the kingdom of Wrenly.

Easy does it, guys...Steady... Steady...

That's it! Perfect!

Always keeping a sharp eye out for the wizard known as **Valos**.

But locating someone so evil, so clever...

WANTED

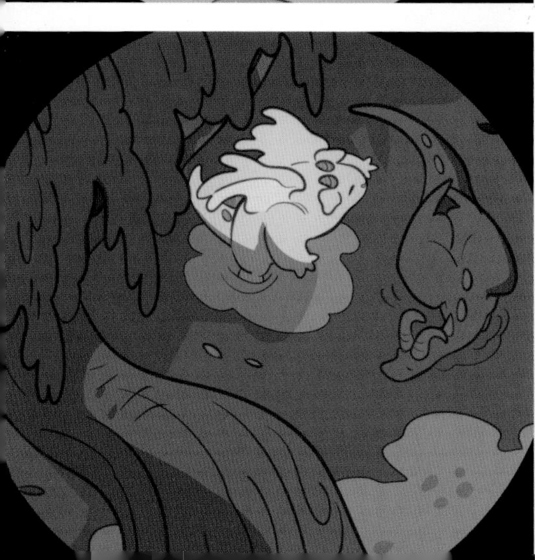

...was proving to be nearly impossible.

And even with the help of their most trusted allies across the kingdom...
Keep searching! Leave no petal unturned!
Ruskin, Roke, and Groth...
...seemed to always be a few steps behind.
Their search came up short in the fairy land of Primlox.

We must keep looking.
Then, the trail went cold in Flatfrost.
CH-CH-CH-CH-CH-CH-CH
Really cold.

WHOOOOOOSH
Buh-bye, dragons!
Fly safe!
We must keep looking.
Yeah, yeah, we heard you, Ruskin. Our tails are frozen, not our ears.
Actually I can't feel my ears. Or my tail. Or my nose. Or my eyelids. Or my claws.

And just when they thought they had a solid lead on where Valos was lurking...

GOTCHA!

...all hope of catching him seemed to vanish into thin air.
FLAP-FLAP-FLAP-FLAP-FLAP-FLAP

While they were in the wizard capital of Hobsgrove, Ruskin made a wild suggestion.
Friends, we need help. I think we should talk to *Grom.*
Even *I* know that's a bad idea!
What? No!
We are chasing a wizard. And that guy, Grom, is a *wizard.* We are literally on a whole island of wizards!
What if Valos put a mind-control spell on him? What if Grom is evil too?

We have to risk it. We have to try. We've lost so much time already.
That's not all you've lost.
GAAAAAH!
Aren't there supposed to be *four* of you? Looks like you've lost someone.
Where is your friend? The orange one?

Her name's Cinder. She's on her own journey this time.

I can sense your sadness. And your fear. No need to be frightened.
Just because I'm a wizard who speaks dragon tongue doesn't mean I'm evil.

Prove it.
How?
Maybe with a peace offering?

Perhaps of the magical snack variety?

MULTIPLY!
Feast, my hungry friend!

They're *not* poisonous, if that's what you're thinking.
How did you know that's what I was thinking?

Duh. I'm magic. Now eat, please.

CHOMP
CHOMP
CHOMP
CHOMP
CHOMP

Thank you for showing us kindness. We should probably take these to go.
We have a lot more ground to cover if we're gonna find Valos.

I wish I could help with your quest, but we have heard nothing.
However, I *can* help with food. Here. For your friend Cinder. Wherever she is.

Oh, I'm sure she's around.

# Chapter 2

Which way?
Which way to...
...Villinelle?

WHOA!

Can you slow down a bit?
Hey, make up your mind! Which way are we going...?
Time out! Amulet, seriously... STOP!
You're a real pain in the neck sometimes, you know that?!

Ha-ha-ha...
...ha-ha-ha!
Who's there? Who's laughing?
Show yourself. I'm in no mood for games.

Hi!

GAAAAAH!!!

FLOOOOOOM

THUD

Oh my! That looked painful.
Trees are for hugging! Not hitting.

Wait a minute...
How many of you are there?
Just one of me, silly!
You can call me *Planks.*

*Planks,* huh? I've never heard such a unique name before.
And I've never seen such a pretty necklace before!

It's more than a necklace. It's...a lot of things.
Trouble is one of them.

Where am I anyway?
Oh no! You bumped your head! Maybe you have *am-ne-sia?*
You...are in... the kingdom... of Wrenly.
I *know* I'm in Wrenly. And I do *not* have amnesia.
I mean, where in Wrenly are we?

You're in *Trellis,* the forest lands.
Are there any dragons here? Anyone who looks like me?
I don't know. I might remember better if you let me hold your necklace.

A pretty please for a pretty necklace! I like shiny things.
I bet it shines in the light just so! Please-please-pleeeeease...

I know the magic word to make it shine brighter than you've ever seen.
And I'll say that word *after* you answer some questions.
Okay, deal!
Are there any shadowy areas around here?
It's a forest. Everywhere is shadowy.

Point taken.

Necklaces don't need shadows to shine.
They need light, silly.

And I know where light is!

NOOOOOO!
SNAP

WAIT! STOP!
FYOOOOOOOM
HELP! I've been robbed by a really cute bug!

Cinder gave chase, but Planks was far too quick.
All Cinder could do was watch helplessly...
...as the little woodland sprite and her amulet...
...were gone in the blink of an eye.

ZOOOOOOOM
Come back!
THWACK
OWWW!
THUD
Come back with my amulet.
Great. This is just great. No amulet. No map. No friends to back me up.
I hope Ruskin and the boys are having more luck than I am.

# Chapter 3

Meanwhile, back near the palace...
...there was a deep rumble in the air.

RUMMMMBLE

Did you hear that?
I think they heard that all the way back on Crestwood.
Yeah. My tummy says I'm gonna faint if I don't get at least eight or nine snacks in it, minimum.
RUMMMMBLE

Better take us to your fancy personal chef, Ruskin, *chop, chop.*
You know you're all banned from the royal kitchen because of *the Midnight Snack* incident.

Don't tell me the kitchen staff is still mad about a *few* crumbs.

SMEAR

KICK

KER-SPLAT

Great.
Did you have to say *crumbs?* I'm starving!
'Scuse me, little ones.
Got a lot o' hungry patrons in there! 'Scuse. Pardon.

Where's that troll headed with all those treats?
Okay, I say we pause our search, take a quick break.
And get our grub on!

What happened next took their breath away. It was an incredible sight, like something from a dream, like a fantasy.
GASP

It's food heaven! The big buffet in the sky!

The trolls from Burth were hosting an epic food fest, and every creature in the kingdom was invited to chow down for free!
If I'm dreaming, don't wake me up. Unless it's for breakfast.

Ruskin, Roke, and Groth were so hungry, they tried one of everything!
Grilled eel rolls with chunky seaweed chili on a sea sponge bun.
EEL ROLL
Moldy vegetable sculptures with swamp sauce.
MOLDY MASTERPIECES
This kinda looks like someone I know. I'll take two!
And of course, frozen bug pops for an after-dinner, sweet treat!
BUGS
Do you want extra eyeballs on that?
Just like Mom used to make!

Bone appetite, my friends!
What's that mean?

I've heard the king say it at dinner.
Pretty sure it means eat everything down to the bone!

CHOMP CHOMP

You know...
CHOMP

CHOMP CHOMP CHOMP
We should have these food fests on Crestwood!

...biggest creatures I ever saw...like monsters... made of lava...

...they had a man with them...
...some kinda **wizard...**

Did you hear that?
Gonna level with you. I can't hear anything over my chewing. These bugs are crunchy.
Shh! Listen.

...and he had hair like...horns, almost. A most peculiar hairstyle for a human.

This human...did he have a long beard? And wear wizard robes?
Where did you see him?!

Say what now?
I said...

Rawr! Rawr, rawr, rawr!
Anyone speak dragon tongue?

Not me.
Nuh-uh.
I barely speak words.

This what you want? Here you go, little fella.
They can't understand us, remember?
Oh *fish-guts!* I always forget that.
A human leading lava monsters around?
Who does that sound like?
C'mon! You know who.

What do you want us to do? We have no idea where that troll saw him.
Or if he even did!

Then we'll follow them! He's gotta say the location sooner or later.
C'mon, let's get stealthy!
Another search mission? But I just sat down to my fourth helping.
Let me finish what's on my plates.
But that'll take forever!

I should have mentioned I'm an eating contest champ. Three years running.
The key to my success? I'm always hungry.

Chapter 4
Far from the sights and smells of the Food Fest...
...something secret was *brewing* in the forest.

A plan.

One that Planks was determined to bring to light.

Huh? What is... that?
Light *from* shadow? How can this be?
It's beautiful.
It's *perfect.*

ZOOOOOM
Planks flew to the light, barely able to see what lay beyond the strange and unusual shimmer.
It glowed.
It dazzled.

SMACK
It *hurt.*
SMOOSH
OW. What strange magic is this?

It's a crystal clear cage that captures light and anything else inside its invisible walls.
Or as we call it on Crestwood: an old *jar*.

Please release me from this shiny prison!
I...uh...I feel faint and dizzy all of a sudden...Something is wrong.
Good try. I put air holes in the top. Because I'm nice.
Unlike you.
What if I make this face?

Nuh-uh. I'm not falling for your cute stuff anymore. You're a thief.

Let me go at once!
Oh, you're free to go anytime you like.
As long as you leave the amulet with me.
I can't! I won't!
Why?
You don't understand. This amulet is not to be trusted.

Huh?
You are not the first to bring this amulet here.
I have seen it before...
Around the neck of a powerful and evil being...

It has no name, but wherever it goes, the wind whispers, ShadowRot.

No amount of warriors or weapons can match the evil forces it summons...

...from *this* cursed stone.
TSSSS
TSSSSS
TSSSS

It's too powerful! We have to fall back and protect the garden!
The little ones will be defenseless!
I was there.
I saw its raw power.

TSSS-ABOOOOM
The forest nearly fell that day.

If this ShadowRot was so all-powerful, how did you stop it?
I mean, the forest is still here. You're here. So what happened?

I...don't know. I wasn't there for the victory.
I went back to protect our homes and our families in case ShadowRot broke through our last line of defense.

Thankfully, it didn't.
The elder sprites managed to banish it *and* the amulet. So the legend says.

Yet now, here it is. And I cannot retreat this time. I must be the one to hide the amulet.
For our safety. And yours.

You'll have to excuse me if I don't completely trust you. Or believe your fairy tale.
I mean, you did just *literally* steal from me like five minutes ago.
Then destroy the amulet yourself!
Or if you cannot destroy it, you can at least hide it.
Hide it away in the most desolate place you can dream of.

I'm sorry I tricked you, but I'm telling the truth now.
I swear it.
Go.

Thank you.

So you'll destroy it then?

No. Not until I find what I'm looking for.
Now stay away from me if you know what's good for ya.

Chapter 5
Meanwhile, far west of the woods, a covered wagon was arriving in Burth, the island of the trolls.

You ain't seen nuthin' like this. Okay, prepare yourselves.
Ta-da! Lava monster!

Huh?
Uhhh...is it invisible?

It was right there, I tells ya! A lava monster, I swear it!
I don't see no lava monster!
For a short guy, you tell a lot of tall tales.

You callin' me a liar?
Yeah, with pants on fire!
Take that back!
They're arguing again?
Yup.
Congratulations. Not only did you pick the smelliest place to hide out, you also picked the worst trolls in all of Wrenly to follow!

Excuse me. A little help here?

My cart's got a wonky wheel and these beets need to go straight to the Food Fest in town!

Lava monsters can wait. No sense in losing a perfectly good batch o' beets!

Sounds like they're going back to the Food Fest!
Groth, focus!
No, I'm saying now's our chance!

Quickly now!
BOING
PLOP
Up in the trees, before they come back!

Now what?
Keep your eyes peeled for any strange lights in the woods.

If there really is a lava monster here, it's going to have to glow eventually.

Nothing glow-y.
What about burny and kinda smoky?

Where?
By that pond. Just over there.

Hmm, could be a campfire.

Or it could be the clue we've been waiting for.
Well, you know what they say. *Where there's smoke...*
...there's marshmallows?

THUD
THUD
THUD

RAWWWRRP
It's a campfire all right...
A campfire with claws.

Wait, it's hurt. Look at its leg.

Any amateur geologist knows... that's black volcanic rock.
The beast must've stepped in the pond and accidentally cooled its own lava.

Good.

Now we know we can use water to fight these things.

I don't know what I'm more shocked by...
...that the troll guy was telling the truth about the lava monster, or that you're happy another creature is suffering!
Seriously, Roke, this is a little dark... even for you.

Well maybe we need to fight darkness with a little darkness, huh?
Or have you both forgotten what's at stake?

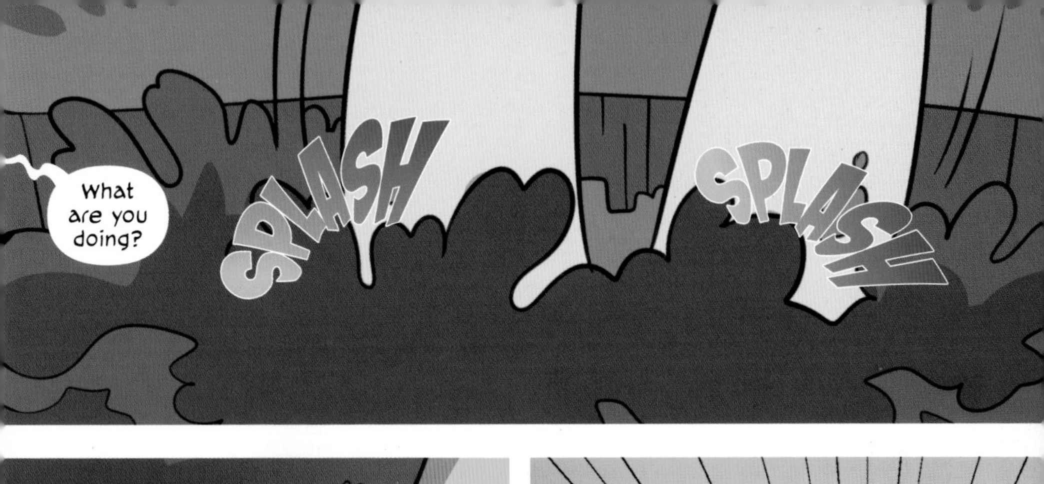
What are you doing?
SPLASH
SPLASH

Getting a location.

RAWWWRRR
Roke, stop!
That's enough! You're scaring it!

Take us to Valos! Do it, or I'll turn you to mud!

ROKE! ENOUGH!

We are not bullies. We are not Valos.
Even if this beast serves him, he's still a living thing that's hurt. And frightened.

We fight the bad guys. We don't act like them.
SPLLLL

I am not going to harm you.
RAWWWRRP
Trust me.

FWOOOSH

FWOOOOSH
FWOOOOSH
RAAAAAWWWWWWR
I hope you know what you're doing!

Thank you.
Hold up. You talk?
What's your name?
Ah-ah.
Nice to meet you, *Ah-ah.*

I'm Ruskin. This is Roke.
And that's Groth.
I'm not apologizing to you, so forget it.
Don't mind him. He's a real sweet dragon when you get to know him.
Where can we find your leader, Ah-ah? Where is Valos?

No. You cannot know this.
THUUUUUUMMP

Stay far away, friendly dragons. Valos is much too dangerous.
Please.

WOW!
Even the lava monsters are afraid of Valos.
What do you suppose that means?

It means we're going to have to be super stealthy...
...when we follow Ah-ah straight to him.

Good to know you're back battling evil again instead of trying to make friends with it.

Oh, I think one evil friend is enough for me.
Wouldn't you agree... *Roke?*
*Awww,* you think I'm evil? You're too kind.

# Chapter 6

As night fell on Wrenly, Cinder found herself journeying down a new path.

So this is my life now? Being led around on a leash like those furry things I've seen on farms.

...outside of their dreams.
Where... am...I?

It's the strangest thing, and I know it's impossible.
But I feel like I've been here before. Somehow.

VRRRRRRRZT

PLIIIIING

VRRRRRRRZT
VRRRRRRRZT

As the amulet touched stone, the night no longer fell...
It *dripped*, coating everything in a thick pool of shadows.

I remember this...

I...
remember...
Only the
amulet...may pass
through...
I have
been here
before!

You did it,
amulet! We found
her! We found...

...VILLINELLE
POOF

Young one... you made it...we don't have much time...
Wait! Before you vanish, we need your help!
Valos is up to something terrible. Something that could lead to many dragons being lost to the After Realm!
If dragon-kind is going to survive, we need you.
I need you.

Touch the amulet...and recite this...incantation...
NOOOO!

I don't understand. Should I touch the amulet or not?

NO, CHILD! You must go!
POOF

Do not listen! She wants to harm you!

LIES!
Go, child! RUN!
I don't know what to do!

There are many lost souls here. Listen only to my voice.
GAAAAAH!
Do not be frightened.

BE frightened!
Leave her alone!

Villinelle? What's going on?!
Go to the amulet...all is well...listen only to my voice...

No, Cinder. Listen to your heart.

You're hurting me! Let go!
Ignite your spark, young one...and repeat after me...

LET...HER ...GO!

CRAAAAAASHHHHH
STOOOM

NOOOOOOO!

Just then the wind carried a voice with it, one that became clear for Cinder in that moment.
Take the amulet and go!

I'm listening to my heart.

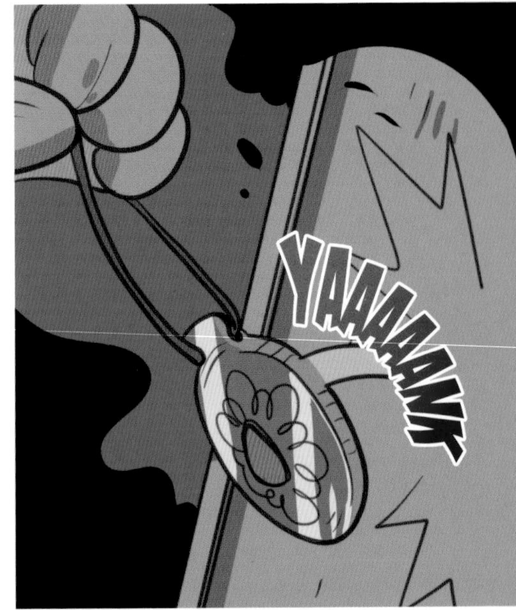
YAAAAANK

And my heart says it's my turn to lead!

I just hope I did the right thing.
You did.

You *listened* to you.

I want it to be you so bad, but I don't know.
Is it really you this time?

FWOOOOOM

Come now, child. We've much to do.
THWOOOOOOSH

I have to warn the others.

# Chapter 7

Back in Burth, the lava hunt was flowing.
Are we sure we saw Ah-ah go this way?

Uh, pretty sure.
SZZZZZLLLE
Why else would this place look like it was hit by a runaway fireball?

I don't get it. There are no ponds in sight, not even so much as a puddle.

And yet, Ah-ah's trail goes completely cold. Right here.
Unless...

He soaked up all the water already...and this pile of rocks is all that's left of him?

Ah-ah, we barely knew you.
You were kind and noble.

Whoa, whoa, Ruskin. That's *not* Ah-ah.
Those aren't even volcanic rocks.

This is just crushed stone from underground.
I see this stuff all the time when I'm digging for new pet rocks.

***Digging!*** Groth, you're a genius!
That's what my mom always tells me!
We lost Ah-ah's trail because he went underground.

Maybe they're all underground?
Start digging!

DIG
DIG
DIG
DIG
DIG

I smell coal...and taste *burning*...
I'm sweating in places I didn't even know I could sweat!

We must be getting close to lava!

I agree. *Very* close.

Underneath Burth, things had been heating up.
Inside the walls of this pit, lava flowed... and somehow *lived*.
They made Lava Beasts. And tamed Lava Dragons.

And as the flames grew, the Lava Creatures grew too.
And like a volcano, they were preparing to break through.

Okay, everyone, just keep cool.
Tough to do when you're inside a literal pit of lava.
I'm scared. We can't stand up to these guys. We're outnumbered.
Exactly why you're going to fly back to Crestwood, Groth.
Warn the others. Tell Ember to send help.
Roke, go back to the surface and set some traps around the perimeter.
Let's make sure nothing can come in...or get out.

I'm gonna get closer and see if I can track Valos down.
Sound like a plan?

Yes, but I much prefer *my* plan.
It starts with capturing three sneaky dragons!
Tie them up!

Hehehe
Teeheehee

How do you like my *Legion of Lava?*

All it took to make them was a spark of pure anger, a touch of greed, and a helping of shadow magic.
All the things I put into that little curse I gave your friend Cinder.

Don't talk about Cinder.
I see my curse worked and your little friend finally went her own way...
...and saw you for what you really are.

A friend?
No. The true heir to the dragon king's throne, of course.
Which makes you a threat to her...but also to me.

You see, Scarlet Dragon, I can't rule the kingdom of Wrenly if someone else has claim to the crown.
And I *will* rule this land. My army will see to that.

And our first plan of attack will be to put that fire inside of you... out.
Then, the palace will fall. And your friends will be my prisoners.
The dragons of Crestwood will join me or face my wrath.
And the kingdom of Wrenly... will be... MINE!

# Chapter 8

Normally, I'd say a situation like this would be tough to swallow...
...but not for the eating contest champ, three years running.
How can you think of food at a time like this?
Okay, okay, I was also thinking about food at a time like this.

What are you getting at, Roke?
You'll see. Groth, show us how you clean your plate!

Now?
Yes, now!

Okay. I just open wide...

Like this...

ERRRRRRR

POP
WHOA! WE'RE FREE!

Hey, Valos!

You told us your plan, now here's ours!

We escape... but not before sending you and your army of lava losers back to the volcano where you belong!

Aren't you glad I packed some extra trick beetles?
SMASH

POOF

NOOOOO!

Roke,
that was
genius!
HOP

*Evil genius!*
The moment Valos
captured us, I knew
he'd blab about his
secret plan.
HOP
Bad guys just
*love* to talk about
their evil plans.

HOP
How
did you
know?
Perks of
being a *little bit*
evil. I know how
bad guys think!

I'm sure
glad to have an
evil friend like
you, buddy!
Yeah, hugs
later. Escape
now!

GET THEM!

RRRROOOOOM

Got any more of those trick beetles?
Yeah, but I don't remember what they all do.

What better time to find out than when we're running for our lives! C'mon!

THWOOOOOSH
Split up and cause as much damage as you can!

FLING
KER-SPLAT

Yes! Bug Juice Beetle! Sticky and cooling!

BONK
Thanks, Roke!

I hope this is one of those exploding beetles!

CRAAAAAACKLE

BOOOOM
AWWW! It was a Birthday Party Beetle!

CRAAAAAASH
Well, don't I feel like a party CRASHER!

Stay back! I've got a beetle here, and I'm not afraid to use it!

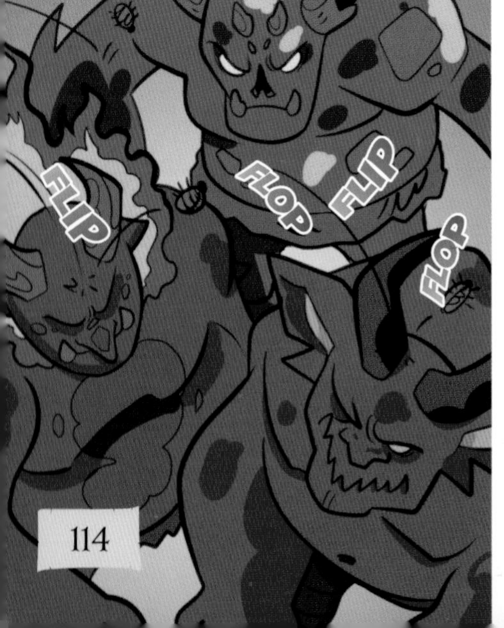
FLIP
FLOP
FLIP
FLOP

What kinda beetles were those?
Just regular beetles.
Awww, C'mon!

ROOOOOOOARRRRRR

LEGION! ATTENTION!

Transform and combine. It is time!

Flow like lava, burn like flame, become one with the darkness as I summon your name!
Rise and awaken from the pits of the earth.
The mighty and ancient...

ERUPT-ORIUS!
RAAAAWWWWWWR

# Chapter 9

Erupt-orius, throw the prisoners in here and let us begin the ritual.

SHOVE

CLANG

Terribly sorry, but I've got to feed my new pet monster.
Would you mind waiting here for...oh I don't know... *THE REST OF YOUR LIVES?!*
*Mu-ah-ha hahaha!*

Before the main course of war, let's kick-start our appetite for destruction!

Might I suggest something *fiery?*
FLAP
FLIP

Okay, new plan.
Yup.

No, I'm asking. What's the new plan?
There isn't one.

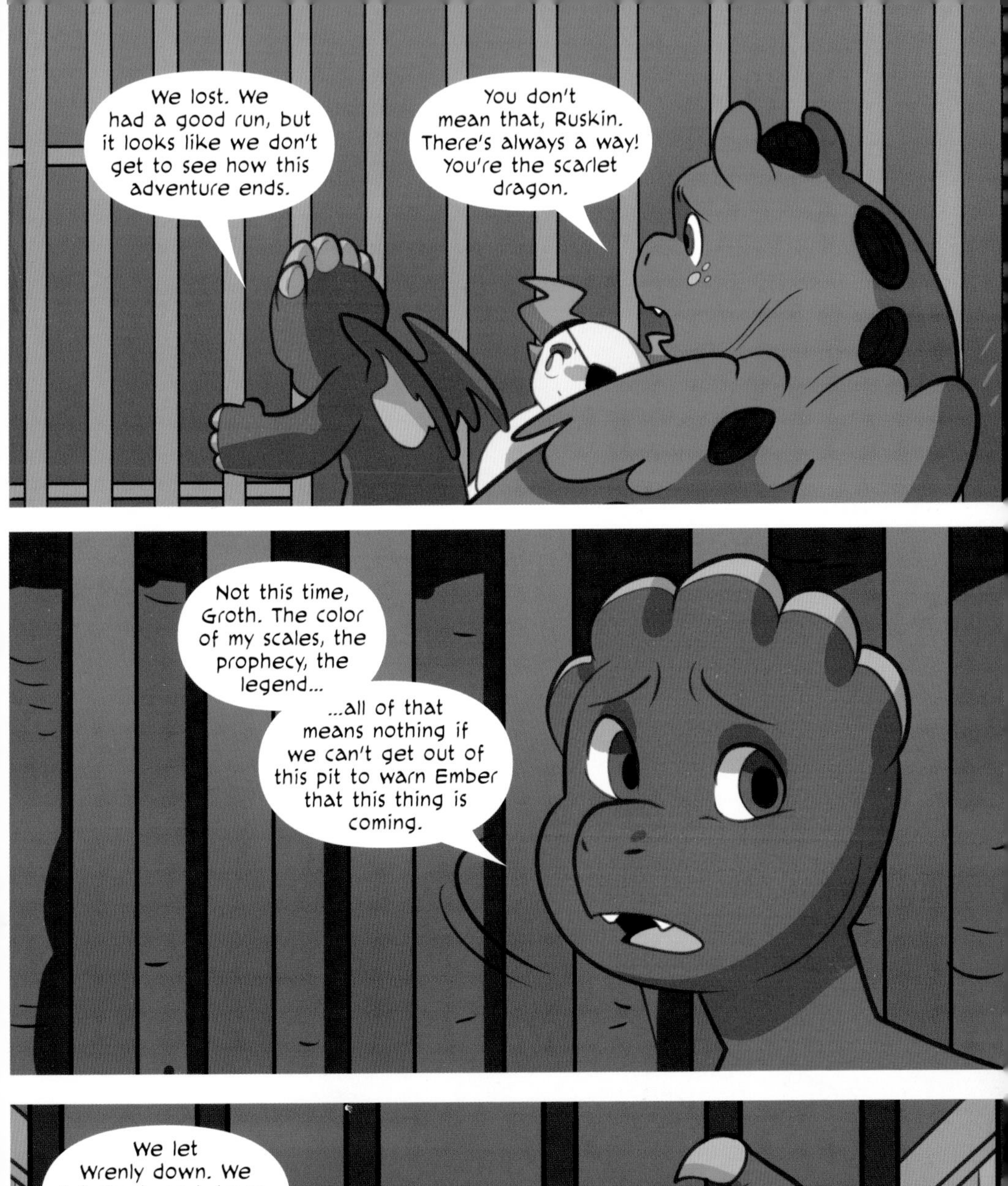
We lost. We had a good run, but it looks like we don't get to see how this adventure ends.
You don't mean that, Ruskin. There's always a way! You're the scarlet dragon.
Not this time, Groth. The color of my scales, the prophecy, the legend...
...all of that means nothing if we can't get out of this pit to warn Ember that this thing is coming.

We let Wrenly down. We let Crestwood down. And worst of all, I let you all down.
I don't see a way out of this. I'm so sorry.

What did you say?

I said, I'm sorry.

You just gave me an idea!

Psssst! Ah-ah! Over here!

Yes! You!

Shhh!

I can't believe I'm about to say this, but...
...I'm sorry.
I'm sorry about how I treated you before. I shouldn't have done that with the water.
I haven't always been treated nicely. It's new for me. My friends are still trying to teach me.
I'm still learning how to be better, how to be good, how to be... kind.
My scarlet friend helped you in the forest. Now please help us.
Please be kind.

QUIET!

Do not speak to my underlings!
SMACK

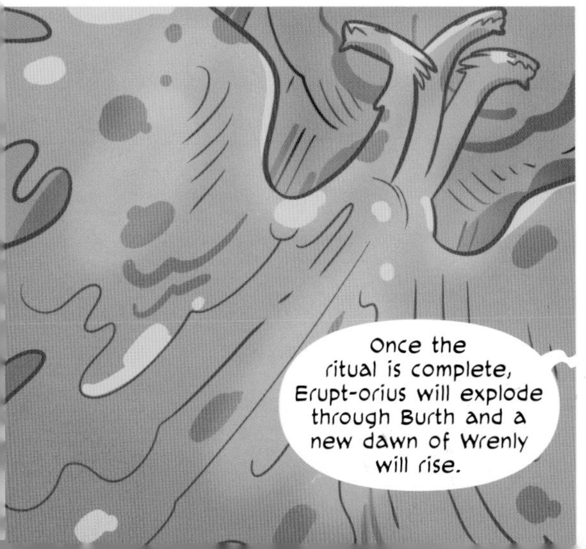
Once the ritual is complete, Erupt-orius will explode through Burth and a new dawn of Wrenly will rise.

WHOOOOA!
PHYOOOM

FLIP
What in the blazes?!

Apology accepted.

TRAITOR!

CLUNK
Go! Now! Warn everyone!

Let's fly!
WHOOOOOOSH

Come with us, Ah-ah! Jump up, I'll grab your hand.

You fizzled fool!
SPLASH

C'mon, Roke! Hurry!

You won't get far, Scarlet Dragon!
The end is here!

# Chapter 10

A dark day dawned on Wrenly.
Haze made the air thick all the way back to **Crestwood.**
It was a rough flight for the dragons.

Thankfully, there was someone there to light their way home.

THUD
THUD

We have so much to tell you!
I have so much to tell you!
Can't wait to hear about your travels!
'Cuz, we love you, but we're on the clock.
There's a giant three-headed Lava Dragon headed this way.
A what now?
We have to speak to your dad immediately!

A few moments later, Ruskin got the dragon elders up to speed.
And then we escaped the lava pit and flew here as quickly as we could.

Roke, sounds like you boys had an intense night.

You have no idea.
I was nice to someone and now they're gone forever. Is this what happens when I'm not evil?
TRICKLE

No dragon seeks out a fight. But if we're going to survive Valos, we have no choice.

We'll need plenty of allies.
That's not all we'll need.

You don't understand. Allies won't be enough. This thing, Erupt-orius, is the biggest dragon I've ever seen.
It has everything but a heart. It won't stop until it devours us all.

It's okay, Ruskin. We also have a magical secret weapon of our own.

VILLINELLE?!

Yes, young ones, it is I. And as thankful as I am to see all of you again...
...there's no time for explanations. Or reunions.

Come, Charron, we've much work to do and no time to do it.
Gather materials and meet me at the hut in the sparkle-field.

How is she?
Is it really her?
But I cried for her at the Shattered Shore!

It's a long story. When this war is over, I'll try to explain.

But for now, let's make sure we stick together!

Deal?

Deal.
Deal.
Deal.

Whoa, Groth! Why is your paw sticky?

Probably from the sugar-bug-sprinkles I had on my ice cream.

Ice cream? I got robbed in the forest and you guys were getting ice cream?
Yeah, we went to a food fest.
It was incredible!
You guys went to a **FOOD FEST** without me?!

A short while later...
Charron! Have you gathered the plants yet?
My Enchantedness, I just want to pick a few more for safety.
You can never be too careful, right?
I couldn't agree more.

Impossible. She has returned?
She has.
And I fear she's not alone.

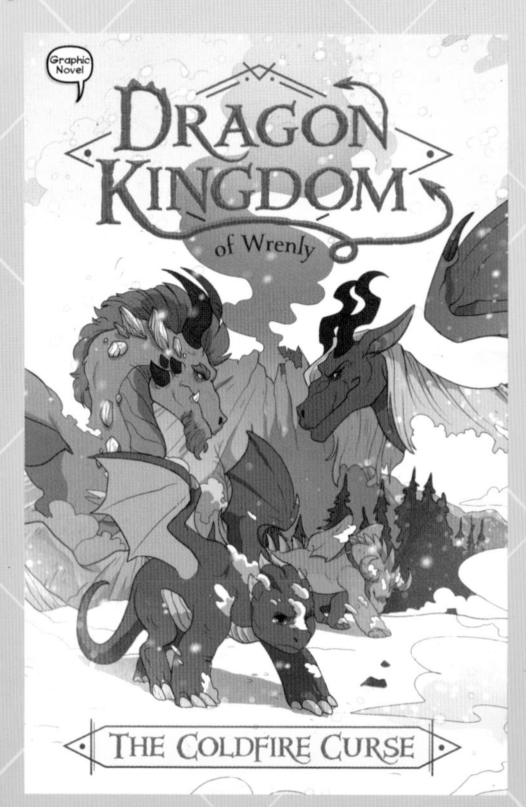
Graphic Novel
DRAGON KINGDOM
of Wrenly
THE COLDFIRE CURSE

Graphic Novel
DRAGON KINGDOM
of Wrenly
SHADOW HILLS

Graphic Novel
DRAGON KINGDOM
of Wrenly
INFERNO NEW YEAR

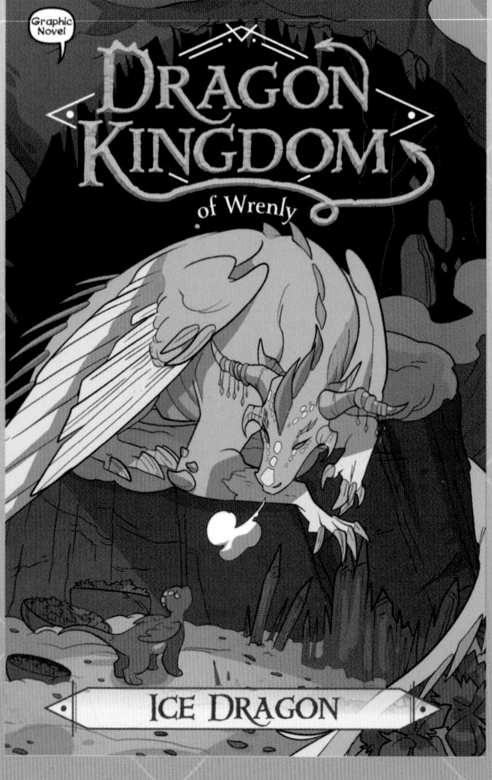
Graphic Novel
DRAGON KINGDOM
of Wrenly
ICE DRAGON

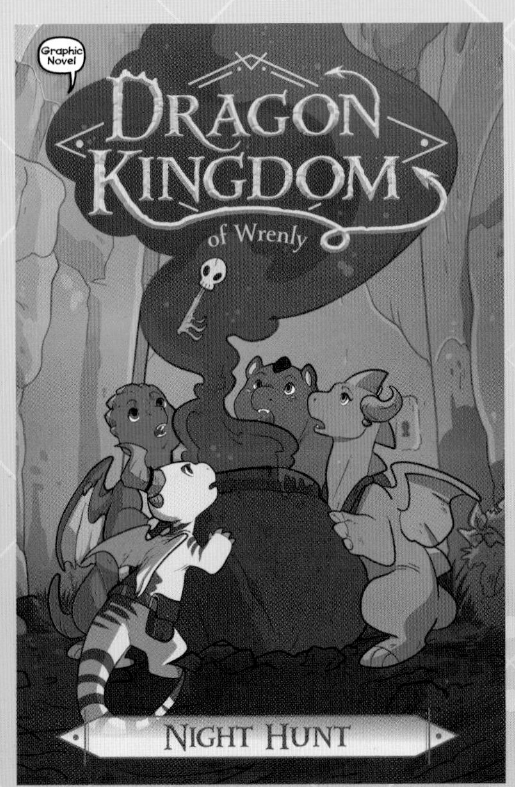
Graphic Novel
DRAGON KINGDOM
of Wrenly
NIGHT HUNT

Graphic Novel
DRAGON KINGDOM
of Wrenly
GHOST ISLAND

Graphic Novel
DRAGON KINGDOM
of Wrenly
CINDER'S FLAME

Graphic Novel
DRAGON KINGDOM
of Wrenly
THE SHATTERED SHORE